Padd'
Painting

MW00945844

Michael Bond

illustrated by David McKee

Collins

One Sunday Paddington was out for a walk with his friend, Mr. Gruber, when they came across some paintings tied to the railings outside a park.

"It's what is known as an 'Outdoor Exhibition'," said Mr. Gruber. "They have one here every week when the weather is nice."

"All the paintings are for sale," Mr. Gruber explained.

"This one is called 'Sunset in Bombay'."

"I'm glad I don't live in Bombay," said Paddington. "It might keep me awake all night."

"How about this one then?" said Mr. Gruber. "It's called 'Storm at Sea'."

Paddington suddenly wished he hadn't eaten such a big breakfast.

"I feel sick," he said, and he hurried on to the next picture.

"This is a portrait of the artist," said Mr. Gruber. "He must have painted it himself because he's signed it."

Paddington gave the picture a hard stare.

"I don't think I shall buy any paintings today, Mr. Gruber," he said.

All the same, Paddington looked very thoughtful as he made his way back home to number thirty-two Windsor Gardens.

When he got there he collected all his paints and brushes from his room and went out into the garden.

Paddington was busy for the rest of that week.

The next Sunday, when he and Mr. Gruber were out for their walk, he led the way back towards Windsor Gardens.

"I'm having an 'Outdoor Exhibition' of my own this week, Mr. Gruber," said Paddington.

"That was meant to be a sunset in Windsor Gardens," said Paddington. "Only I'm afraid it took me rather a long time and it got dark before I was able to finish it."

"And that's a picture of a rainstorm, only it got very wet and all the paint ran."

"This is my *best* one," said Paddington. "It's a picture of me. I've put my special paw mark on to show I painted it myself."

Mr. Gruber gazed at Paddington's portrait for a long time.

"It is very good, Mr. Brown," he said at last, not wishing to upset his friend, "but I think you look even better in real life."

"I kept going upstairs to look at myself in the mirror," said Paddington, "but by the time I got downstairs again I'd forgotten what I looked like.

"Painting isn't as easy as it looks," he added sadly, "especially with paws. I think I may give up."

It was Mr. Gruber's turn to look thoughtful. "I hope you don't do that, Mr. Brown," he said.

After Mr. Gruber had said goodbye,
Paddington sat down beside his paintings
hoping that someone would stop and buy
one.

But it was a warm day and no one came
past. In the end he fell asleep.

When he awoke, Paddington found to his surprise that all his pictures had gone.

But tucked inside his duffle coat he found an envelope with his name on:
Mr. Paddington Brown, 32 Windsor Gardens.
And inside the envelope there was some money and a note saying "Thank you".

If Mr. and Mrs. Brown recognized Mr. Gruber's writing they didn't say anything, which was very wise of them.

They hadn't had such a peaceful time for ages.

Mr. Gruber was pleased at being able to help his friend.

And best of all, Paddington carried on painting.

So everyone was happy.

"I think I may paint a *family* portrait today,"
said Paddington. "That is, if I have enough
paint left for all the smiles."